SALLY PLAYING IN THE SHADOWS

By Hanny Morag

Thanks to my kids who inspired my stories

Thanks to my husband, who was always
there to support me.

Thank you, dear reader, for choosing to
read my book,

INTRODUCTION

Fear is real but not overpowering.

Only what you allow to hunt you can become

a source of terror to you.

How scary can the dark be?

How tormenting can the shadows of darkness be?

Can you overcome the torment and the fear that comes with it?

This is something you can never know

until you try.

At night before bed,
In Sally's room, he noticed some trails
Shadows and lights began to penetrate.
Casting scary figures and shapes

At first, Sally was so scared,
Under his blanket, he trembled and babbled.

He shouted "Mommyyyyyy
The walls have me startled."

From the wall crawled out a big and scary witch,
As cruel as a bandit.

Her long nails point out like a tiger with rage.
She wants to split me up like a cake

and put me in a fridge.

Sally shouted, "Mommy come. Save me! Save me!

She's trying to eat me up like dinner
If you don't hurry my Blood will be shed
It will be a disaster if I am dead.

"MOMMY COME.
SAVE ME!"

Sally's mom rushed to the room without hesitating.
Did she find herself amidst a situation so terrifying?

Let's see. She said "Oh my sweet and dear Sally,
it is nothing at all
This is just a shadow cast on the wall."

Here, I'll sit right by your side,

And I'll find you a story about this.
Let's look at the shadows once again.
And see the scary nature of the bogeyman.

So Mom and Sally opened their eyes.

Let's look at the shadows together.
We would be able to identify them better
This horror scenes, we can't fight without each other.

Slowly on the wall, a shadow crept in,
An incredibly black yet beautiful cat.

Her furs become amazing as her eyes shine,
A hollow eyes without neither sound nor whine.

Sally showed no fears at all,
He obviously loves this cat crawling on his wall.

Lines and shapes were at the appropriate place,
Mommy is it perhaps a mantis with lovely glace

Lines and shapes are not so nasty,
Figures and Shapes of people move not so hasty.

Sally has no fears about them at all,
Sally loves these figures, crawling on his wall.

One man is round and a little chubby
Another man, Looks a bit like a scarecrow

Shadows, nose, and eyes were in a perfect row,
A complete celebration come and go.

Sally has no fears about them at all,
As he loves this celebration, and crawling on his wall.

As his mom walked out of his room and turned
off the light,

He was not afraid at all.
He was already a hero.
He looked amused at the shadows grew deep.
He started until he fell asleep.

You see,
Sally has no fears about the shadows at all,
Sally loves to dream of nice shadows,
crawling on his wall.
I am sure,

you have all learned the game from Sally.

Do you also see shadows,

dancing for you, on the walls?

Do you see similar characters every night?
Be calm,

and know,

that this game will pass if you turn on the light.

There is no need to be afraid of shadows at all,
It's only a nice game looking for images in the shadows,
crawling on your wall.

THE END

Did you like the story?

SALLY PLAYING IN THE SHADOWS

Please give me a review on Amazon,

and follow my Amazon Author Page

for more Books:

https://amzn.to/2X6OszP

Thank you for you purchase!

You're welcome to enjoy free stories at my site:

/https://www.hmstories.com

As a bonus for buying this book you will also get a

25% off purchase coupon: **CHARM25**

At my Etsy Store- There you will find

A High-quality PDF Digital Product as a PRINT file

FOR Download and print at home!
ALL

Based on ILLUSTRATIONS from my stories

Full with adorable Characters and Scenery from in the story.

And cute SVG file.

This is the link to the coloring pages:

https://etsy.me/2UtIqIc

This is the link to the SVG file:

https://etsy.me/2XfKQft

In addition, You and your child can enjoy free jingles on my YouTube channel

This is the link for the Charming Monster jingle:
https://www.youtube.com/watch?v=uWuIKGp9Xx4